PUFFIN BOOKS

The Puffin Book of Stories for Five-Year-Olds

Wendy Cooling was educated in Norwich and, after a short time in the Civil Service, spent time travelling the world. On her return to England she trained as a teacher, went on to teach English in London comprehensive schools for many years and was for a time seconded as an advisor on libraries and book-related work in schools. She left teaching to work on the promotion of books and reading as Head of the Children's Book Foundation (now Booktrust), and later founded Bookstart, the national programme that helps to bring books to young readers. She continues to work with the programme as a consultant, as well as working as a freelance book consultant and reviewer.

Other books edited by Wendy Cooling

THE PUFFIN BOOK OF STORIES FOR SIX-YEAR-OLDS

THE PUFFIN BOOK OF STORIES FOR SEVEN-YEAR-OLDS

THE PUFFIN BOOK OF STORIES FOR EIGHT-YEAR-OLDS

THE PUFFIN BOOK OF CHRISTMAS STORIES

D IS FOR DAHL

The Puffin Book of

Stories for 5 Five-Year-Olds

Edited by Wendy Cooling

Illustrated by Steve Cox

PUFFIN

PUFFIN BOOKS

Published by the Penguin Group
Penguin Books Ltd, 80 Strand, London WC2R 0RL, England
Penguin Group (USA) Inc., 375 Hudson Street, New York, New York 10014, USA
Penguin Group (Canada), 90 Eglinton Avenue East, Suite 700, Toronto, Ontario, Canada M4P 2Y3
(a division of Pearson Penguin Canada Inc.)
Penguin Ireland, 25 St Stephen's Green, Dublin 2, Ireland (a division of Penguin Books Ltd)
Penguin Group (Australia), 250 Camberwell Road, Camberwell, Victoria 3124, Australia
(a division of Pearson Australia Group Pty Ltd)
Penguin Books India Pvt Ltd, 11 Community Centre, Panchsheel Park, New Delhi – 110 017, India
Penguin Group (NZ), 67 Apollo Drive, Mairangi Bay, Auckland 1310, New Zealand
(a division of Pearson New Zealand Ltd)
Penguin Books (South Africa) (Pty) Ltd, 24 Sturdee Avenue, Rosebank, Johannesburg 2196, South Africa

Penguin Books Ltd, Registered Offices: 80 Strand, London WC2R 0RL, England

penguin.com

First published 1996
043

The Acknowledgements on pages 121–3 constitute an extension of this copyright page

Set in 16/18pt Monophoto Ehrhardt
Made and printed in England by Clays Ltd, St Ives plc

British Library Cataloguing in Publication Data
A CIP catalogue record for this book is available from the British Library

ISBN: 978–0–140–37458–2

www.greenpenguin.co.uk

Contents

Introduction

The stories in this collection, some old and some new, are for sharing, enjoying and talking about. If there's one that really works for you and your children, look for more books by the same author and even for more stories about the same character. Stories, of course, cross age groups but the ones in this book have all been tried out and enjoyed by five-year-olds.

Reading with young children is a source of great pleasure and delight and this early reading helps to develop the imagination and an ear for language. Reading time is not always a quiet time as children want to talk, ask questions and become really involved in the story. Sometimes they will listen in silent wonder for a time, but generally children will want to share the experience of the story with you. As they begin to recognize the stories they will join in even more – children love the familiar so don't be suprised to be reading the same story again and again.

The stories in this book don't take long to read and are ideal for those spare ten minutes at any time of the day. Make reading a part of every day and enjoy the experience with your children.

Wendy Cooling

Eric's Elephant

JOHN GATEHOUSE

Eric had always wanted a pet of his own.

"A cat," Eric thought, as he wandered around the Church Jumble Sale. "Or a hamster. Or a rabbit would be nice."

He bought a raffle ticket from the man behind the White Elephant stall.

Eric hoped he would win something. He had never won anything before. But today he did.

"You win first prize!" cried the man behind the stall.

He handed Eric a rope. Tied to the

other end was an honest-to-goodness, real, live, white elephant.

"I can't take an elephant home!" said Eric. "My mum will go bonkers!"

"You won her. She's all yours now," the man said.

Eric led his elephant out of the church grounds and down the street. Passers-by stared in surprise as they went along.

"I've always wanted a pet," Eric said. "But I'm not quite sure you were what I had in mind."

Eric's elephant didn't answer.

She was too busy munching through the box of bananas standing outside Mr Sprout's vegetable shop.

"Hey! Those bananas cost money!" shouted Mr Sprout crossly. "Wait until I tell your mum, Eric!"

"Did you have to do that?" sighed Eric gloomily, leading his elephant away. "Mum will go twice as bonkers when she hears about this."

Eric's elephant didn't answer.

She had stopped to eat up Mrs

Groggins' prize flower-patch.

Then she sat down for a rest on PC Crumble's garden fence. It creaked and groaned and slowly fell apart.

Eric wondered how many times in one day his mum could go bonkers.

When they reached home, Eric could hear his mum in the kitchen. She was busy trying to mend the vacuum cleaner. Eric didn't think she sounded in a very good mood.

"SSSSSSSSSH!" Eric whispered to his elephant. "I don't think I'll show you to Mum just now."

Eric pushed his elephant through the front door. It was a tight squeeze.

Just as Eric was about to give up trying, POP!, his elephant fell into the hall.

Eric led his elephant up the stairs. With another squeeze he pushed her into his bedroom.

"Perhaps I could hide you under my bed," said Eric.

Eric's elephant didn't answer. She was too busy dancing to the music coming from Eric's radio.

"ERIC! WHAT ARE YOU DOING?" shouted his mum. "It sounds like there's a herd of elephants up there!"

"No, there isn't," said Eric. "There's only one."

"Don't be cheeky, Eric," said his mum, coming into his room.

She saw the elephant sitting on Eric's bed. Her eyes widened and her throat made a funny gurgling noise.

"ERIC! GET IT OUT OF HERE!" screamed Eric's mum at the top of her voice.

Leading his elephant by her trunk, Eric took her back downstairs again.

Eric didn't think things could get any worse. Then Mr Sprout, Mrs Groggins and PC Crumble arrived. So did Eric's dad. And Eric knew things were about to become much worse.

"Eric, what is going on?" asked his dad, staring at the elephant and all the angry people.

Eric tiptoed out of the house with his elephant, while his dad listened to the terrible tales Mr Sprout, Mrs Groggins and PC Crumble had to tell.

"I've gone off pets," said Eric.

Eric's elephant didn't answer. She was too busy watching the long queue of cars lined up outside Mr Sprocket's garage.

The drivers looked very hot and angry.

"Everyone wants to wash their cars," explained Mr Sprocket. "But my Car Wash machine has broken down."

Eric had an idea. He filled up a large bucket with water from the garage tap. He told his elephant to suck the water up in her trunk.

Eric pointed the elephant's trunk at one of the cars.

"FIRE!" shouted Eric, and his elephant blew very hard. The water squirted out of her trunk and SPLAAASSSH! all over the car.

Eric's elephant did the same with all the other cars. Then Eric wiped off the water with a cloth. When he had finished the cars were sparkling clean.

"Well done!" said one of the drivers. He

patted Eric on the head and his elephant on her trunk.

One by one the drivers paid Eric for cleaning their cars. Soon he had collected a lot of money.

"Now I've got enough money to repay everyone for all the damage my elephant caused," grinned Eric.

Eric took his elephant back home. His mum was not very pleased to see them.

"My vacuum cleaner's broken. I can't clean the carpet and my friends will soon be arriving for tea," she said. "And to make matters worse, you bring home an elephant!"

"Don't worry, Mum," said Eric. "My elephant can help you. She's very useful."

Eric led the elephant into the living room. Eric's mum watched in astonishment as the elephant sucked up all the dust and dirt in her trunk and then blew it into the rubbish bin. Then Eric's elephant vacuumed the curtains, dusted the sideboard and got rid of the giant cobweb in the corner of the room.

"What a clever elephant," said Eric's mum, giving the elephant a kiss. "She's not such a useless lump after all."

Eric found his dad in the garden watering the flowers with a small watering-can.

"My elephant will do it," said Eric.

Eric's elephant sprayed the garden with water from her trunk. Then she sprayed Eric, just for fun.

"Ha, ha! Your elephant can water the neighbours' gardens too," said Eric's dad. "Then they won't have anything to complain about."

"And she can live in our shed," suggested Eric. "She can't get into any trouble then."

"TOOT! TOOT!" answered Eric's elephant with a loud trumpet. She liked this idea best of all.

The Special, Special Trainers!

MALORIE BLACKMAN

Betsey peered in through the shoe shop window. There they were! Her special trainers. Her magic trainers. With those trainers she wouldn't just run, she'd *fly*! No one would be able to catch her in those extra special, *special* trainers.

"Betsey, come away from that window." Granma Liz frowned.

"Oh Granma Liz. Look! The trainers I was telling you about – they're still there!"

Betsey pointed.

"They're going to stay there too!" Granma Liz said. "Come on."

"But I need a new pair of trainers," said Betsey. "Mine are worn to nothing now."

"I don't know how you can get through the soles of your shoes so fast," Granma Liz tutted. "You must be eating them!"

"Granma Liz, just look at these trainers. Look at those colours. Look at the laces. Look at the . . ."

"Look at the time!" Granma Liz glanced down at her watch. "Come on Betsey, or we'll miss our bus."

"But Granma Liz . . ."

"Betsey, for the last time, I'm not buying you those trainers. For weeks now all your mam and I have heard from you is trainers this and trainers that!"

"But Granma Liz, my best friend May has a pair of those trainers," Betsey said eagerly, "and you should see her when she runs. She doesn't run, she soars and swoops – just like a bird or a plane."

"Betsey, you talk some real nonsense sometimes," said Granma Liz. "Come on, child."

So Betsey had to leave the front of the shoe shop. She crossed her fingers tight, tight, tight.

"I want those trainers something fierce," Betsey muttered to herself.

"What did you say, Betsey?" asked Granma Liz.

"Nothing, Granma," said Betsey.

"Hhmm!" said Granma. "Hhmm!" And without another word, off they went home.

But on the way home, Betsey had an idea . . .

At dinner time, the family sat around the table. Granma Liz and Betsey and Sherena, Betsey's bigger sister and Desmond, Betsey's bigger brother. For dinner there was cou-cou and flying fish and salad and a huge jug of delicious soursop drink mixed with milk and plenty of ice. Betsey licked her lips. Scrumptious!

"Pass the salt please, Betsey," said Sherena.

Betsey picked up the glass salt shaker. "The tops of the trainers I want are just as white as this salt," said Betsey.

She pointed to the pepper bottle.

"And the soles of the trainers I want are blacker than the writing on the pepper bottle." Sherena and Desmond looked at each other.

"Betsey, I want to hear no more about those trainers. D'you hear?" frowned Granma Liz.

"Yes, Granma," Betsey said. Betsey poured herself a glass of soursop drink, but some spilt on to the sky-blue tablecloth. The white liquid spread out.

"Betsey!" said Granma Liz. "Look at that mess."

"That stain is just about the size of the trainers I want," Betsey murmured.

Granma Liz could stand it no longer.

"Elizabeth Ruby Biggalow, all day, all week, all *month*, you've done nothing but mope and whine about those trainers," frowned Granma Liz. "Your long face is spoiling my day as well as my dinner. Now not another word."

And Betsey knew then that she'd better shut up. Whenever Granma Liz called her by her whole, full name, Betsey knew she was treading dangerously close to trouble.

But for the rest of the evening all Betsey had in her head were her special trainers. She even fell asleep dreaming of soaring and flying, her special trainers on her feet.

The next morning, when Betsey went down for breakfast, everyone was unusually quiet.

"What's the matter?" asked Betsey.

"I've got something for you." Mam smiled. "As your old trainers are in such a state I decided to get you some new ones."

"You bought the trainers!" Betsey couldn't believe it.

"Now perhaps we can all get some peace," Granma Liz sniffed.

Betsey grinned and grinned. Her extra special trainers. She'd got them at last. Mam handed over the bag she was hiding behind her back. Betsey opened the bag and . . .

"What's the matter?" asked Sherena.

"Oh!" Betsey couldn't say anything else. Her eyes started stinging and there was a huge, choking lump in her throat. Botheration! These weren't the trainers she wanted. Where were the ones with the white fronts and the black soles and the red laces? Where were her special trainers? Still in the shop – that's where!

These ones were pink and grey and didn't have any black writing on them like the ones she wanted.

"Betsey . . ." Granma Liz warned. "Your mam had to take time off work to buy those for you."

"Don't you like them, Betsey?" Mam asked.

"They're lovely," Betsey whispered.

"Put them on then," urged Desmond.

Betsey sat down and, oh so slowly she put on her new shoes.

"They look boss!" smiled Sherena.

"The best trainers I've ever seen," said Desmond.

Granma Liz didn't say anything. She just watched Betsey.

"Can I go and show them to my friend May please?" Betsey asked Mam.

"Go ahead then," she smiled. "But don't stay with her too long. You've still got your morning chores to finish."

Betsey ran out of the kitchen. She couldn't wait to get out of the house. She looked down at her feet. These shoes weren't her special trainers. These shoes were just horrible. Betsey ran all the way to May's house – sprinting as if to sprint the trainers right off her feet. At May's house, Betsey knocked and knocked again. May opened the door. Worse still, May opened the door wearing the very same trainers that Betsey wanted so much.

"Hi May," Betsey said glumly.

"Hi Betsey," said May. "I was just going to the beach. Coming?"

Betsey shrugged. "Just for a little while."

So off they went. But things weren't right. No, they weren't. By the time Betsey and May reached the beach they were having a full blown, full grown argument.

"Well, my trainers are the best in the country," said May.

"My trainers are the best in the world," Betsey fumed.

"Talk sense! My trainers are the best in the universe," said May.

"I hate you and your trainers," Betsey shouted. "And I hate these ones I'm wearing and I hate *everything*."

"And I hate you and your smelly shoes too," May stormed.

Betsey and May stared and glared and scowled and glowered at each other.

Then Betsey started to smile, then to laugh, then to hold her stomach she was laughing so much.

"What's so funny?" May asked, still annoyed.

"Botheration! Imagine hating a pair of shoes!" Betsey laughed. "You hate my shoes and I hate your shoes. And both pairs of shoes are probably laughing at us for being so foolish."

"All this fuss over a pair of trainers," May agreed with a giggle.

"Come on! Let's have a run. Things are always better after a run on the beach," said Betsey. "I'll race you to that palm tree yonder."

"Ready . . . Set . . . Go . . ."

And off they both sprinted, faster than fast. They leapt over the sand and through the lapping water, kicking up the spray as they went, laughing and laughing. Until finally they both collapsed in the shade of the palm tree Betsey had pointed to. Who won the race? Neither May nor Betsey cared.

Betsey glanced down at her wet shoes. They were all right! Not the ones she'd wanted, but a present from her mam just the same. A special present. A wonderful surprise.

"Look at that!" said May, surprised. May pointed to her trainers. The red colour in her laces was running down the white front of her trainers and over the black writing. May's trainers didn't like getting wet – not one little bit. Betsey glanced down at her own trainers still grey and pink and no running colours anywhere. She jumped up.

"May, let's walk along the beach for a bit longer," said Betsey. "We can collect shells and paddle. Never mind our trainers. Let's walk along in our bare feet."

"Yeah! It's much nicer walking on the sand in bare feet anyway," May agreed.

And May and Betsey ran over the white sand and through the blue water, their trainers knotted at the laces and dangling around their necks.

The Lonely Lion

JOHN GRANT

Zak lived in a very old house. Some people said that it was haunted! Certainly there were some very strange sounds to be heard from time to time, particularly at night.

Sometimes it was the wind in the chimneys. Sometimes it was owls perched hooting on the roof. Sometimes the noises made Zak's hair stand on end, and he didn't like to think what those were!

One night Zak was wakened by a very mysterious noise. It wasn't the wind. It wasn't . . . well, it didn't make his hair stand on end. And it didn't come from the roof or the chimneys.

It came from the garden!

Zak got out of bed and slipped on his dressing-gown. He opened the window and looked down into the moonlit garden. Two huge yellow eyes looked straight back up at him.

Zak banged the window shut and shook with fright.

The noise came again. Someone – or something – was crying!

Plucking up his courage, Zak opened the window again. Looking up, and sobbing as though its heart would break, was an enormous lion. Tears rolled down its nose, and it wiped them away with a paw the size of a soup plate.

"Please, can I come in?" said the lion in a sniffly voice. "I'm lost and cold."

Zak went downstairs and very nervously opened the front door.

"C-c-come in," he said, "if you are lost and cold."

"I'm hungry, too," said the lion, with a

look at Zak that made him more nervous than ever.

"I'm not sure that I have any lion food," said Zak.

"A slice of toast and a cup of tea will do nicely," said the lion.

It followed Zak into the kitchen where he put some wood on the fire, and the lion sat down to warm itself while Zak filled the kettle.

"Very nice," said the lion after a while, brushing toast crumbs from its whiskers. "You just don't get toast where I've come from."

"Where's that?" asked Zak. "Africa?"

"Wigan," said the lion. "Wigan Safari Park. I couldn't stand it a minute longer. I could have screamed with boredom. I did one day. Or, at least, I roared. And . . . there were complaints."

"Who from?" asked Zak.

"From the visitors because I frightened them. And from the other lions because I woke them up. There's nothing to do in a safari park but eat and sleep."

"How did you get to *be* in a safari park?" asked Zak.

"It's a long story," said the lion. "I used to perform in Lord Jim's Royal Circus. I had a partner, Bert Ramsbottom. We were Captain Heroic and his Man-Eating Lion. Bert wore his Captain Heroic uniform, and I roared and snarled when he cracked his whip. Then I would leap up on to a little platform and sort of cringe, while the people cheered and clapped Captain Heroic for being so brave. It wasn't easy, I can tell you!"

"What wasn't?" asked Zak.

"Keeping a straight face," said the lion. "Trying to look fierce and not to laugh. Because it was all really rather silly. Bert and I were the best of friends. And I do miss him."

The lion sniffed again and wiped his eyes.

"We always finished the act with Bert putting his head in my mouth. I didn't like that bit. His hairspray tasted awful! And I didn't like it when I had to do silly tricks like walking on my front paws and turning cartwheels. Still, we were a great act, until . . ."

"Until what?" asked Zak.

"A man from the council came one day to see Lord Jim. They didn't like circuses, particularly animal acts. Lord Jim's Royal Circus closed down. I was retired. I don't know what happened to Bert. And I miss him terribly, and the music, and the applause." And the lion began to cry once more. Then it wiped its eyes and said, "Now, if you don't mind, I'd like to sleep." And it curled up in front of the fire and started to snore.

Zak went back to bed and fell asleep wondering what on earth he was going to do with a runaway lion who had been in showbiz!

When he woke in the morning, Zak hoped that perhaps it had all been a dream, but the lion was sitting in the kitchen when he went down.

"How about a spot of breakfast, then?" it said.

They sat down with bowls of cornflakes.

"I rather hoped you might have Rice Krispies," said the lion. "I like listening to them."

Over toast and coffee, Zak introduced himself.

"Pleased to meet you, Zak," said the lion. "I'm called Wallace, after an ancestor of mine. He was famous in his day. He lived in Blackpool Zoo, and they say he ate a boy called Albert. It was never proved."

Zak switched on the radio. There was a brass band playing.

"That's my music!" cried Wallace. "'Entry of the Gladiators'," and he leapt up, knocking over the table and scattering the breakfast things in all directions.

"I'll show you my act!" he cried. "Although it won't be the same without Bert – I mean Captain Heroic."

"Let's go outside," said Zak. And he hurriedly opened the front door before Wallace did any more damage.

And there, on the lawn in front of Zak's house, Wallace put on a show.

"Not the same without Bert and the man-eating lion bit," he explained, "but I'll show you some of the old silly tricks." And it was most entertaining all the same as Wallace walked on his back paws, then on his front paws, did somersaults, and turned cartwheels.

As he finished, there was a chorus of chirps, coos, mews, barks and whistles. Four pigeons, a flock of sparrows, two stray cats and the Yorkshire terrier from next door had come to watch.

Wallace bowed low. Then he blew kisses to the audience. "Thank you! Thank you! Bless you!" he cried, while the tears rolled down his cheeks again.

He's overdoing it a bit, thought Zak, but before he could think any further there was an interruption.

A crowd of men rushed on to the lawn. "There he is!" they shouted. "Don't panic! Stay still everybody!"

"What do you mean?" shouted Zak. "And who are you anyway?"

"It's all right!" they shouted back. "We

know how to deal with dangerous wild animals."

"Don't be silly!" said Zak. "It's only Wallace. He's my friend, and my guest. And, what's more, you are trespassing!"

"We are from Wigan Safari Park," said the man who seemed to be in charge. "Your friend ran away. He has caused, I may say, considerable inconvenience!"

At that, Wallace started to cry again. His lip trembled as he sobbed, "Don't let them take me back there! Let me stay!"

"I'd like to," said Zak. "But I don't really have accommodation for lions . . . particularly lions who are stars. But I do have an idea. You go back quietly to the safari park and, if my idea works out, everything will end happily."

So Wallace went with the men to where they had parked their truck. He climbed into the back and the audience waved him goodbye.

Zak hurried into the house. In the phone book he found an entry for the Society of Circus Performers. He spoke to a friendly lady who said, "Ramsbottom? I don't think –"

"His other name is Captain Heroic," said Zak.

"Of course," said the lady, and she gave Zak Bert's address at the Home for Retired Lion-tamers.

Zak wrote a letter:

Dear Mr Ramsbottom,

You don't know me, but I am a friend of Wallace the Man-Eating Lion, and I have a plan . . .

He wrote another letter, this time to the Manager of Wigan Safari Park.

Meanwhile back at the safari park Wallace was as bored as ever. Until, one day, the manager drove up in his jeep that was painted to look like a zebra. He had a passenger. "Wallace!" called the manager, "I have a visitor for you."

A bald-headed gentleman got down. Wallace looked. No . . . it couldn't be! Yes! It was!

"Bert!" he cried. And the two of them hugged each other while the tears rolled down their checks, and the other lions looked on in astonishment. The manager said, "Mr Albert Ramsbottom is to be the safari park's new lion expert." Then he drove off again, leaving Bert and Wallace grinning at each other.

Zak paid a visit to Wigan Safari Park. He met Bert, who told him that one of his ancestors had been eaten by a lion at Blackpool so lion-taming was, in a manner of speaking, in his blood.

The two friends are still happily together at Wigan and every year on Zak's birthday, they pay him a visit. There on the lawn in front of the house they put on their act. Bert cracks his whip. Wallace roars and cringes . . . then winks at the audience to show that it is all in fun. And as Bert is bald and doesn't use hairspray Wallace doesn't mind when he puts his head in his mouth. To the great delight of Zak and the pigeons, sparrows, stray cats, and the Yorkshire terrier from next door.

The King with Dirty Feet

An Indian tale

POMME CLAYTON

Once upon a time there was a king. He lived in a hot, dusty village in India. He had everything he wanted and was very happy. But there was one thing that this king hated and that was bathtime.

Perhaps he was a little bit like you?

This king had not washed for a week, he had not washed for a month, he had not washed for a whole year. He had begun to smell. He smelt underneath his arms, in between his toes, behind his ears and up his nose. He was the smelliest king there has ever been. His servants were all very polite about it, but nobody liked to be in the same room as him. Until one day the smell became too much for even the king himself, and he said rather sadly, "I think it is time I had a bath."

He walked slowly down to the river. The villagers whispered, "The king's going to have a bath!" and they rushed down to the river bank to get the best view.

Everyone fell silent when the king stepped into the cool, clear river water. When he called for the royal soap, a huge cheer arose. He washed himself from top to bottom, scrubbed his hair and brushed his teeth. He played with his toy ducks and his little boat.

Then, at last, when he was quite clean, he called for the royal towel and stepped out of the river.

When he had finished drying himself he saw that his feet were covered with dust.

"Oh bother," he cried. "I forgot to wash them." So he stepped back into the water and soaped them well. But as soon as he stood on dry land his feet were dirty again.

"Oh my goodness," he said crossly. "I didn't wash them well enough. Bring me a scrubbing brush." The king scrubbed his feet until they shone. But still, when he stepped on the ground they were dirty.

This time the king was furious. He shouted for his servant, Gabu. Gabu came running and bowed low before the king.

"Gabu," boomed the king, "the king has had a bath, the king is clean, but the earth is dirty. There is dust everywhere. You must clean the earth so there is no more dust and my feet stay clean."

"Yes, Your Majesty," replied Gabu.

"You have three days in which to rid the land of dust, and if you fail do you know what will happen to you?" asked the king.

"No, Your Majesty."

"ZUT!" cried the king.

"ZUT?" said Gabu. "What is ZUT?"

"ZUT is the sound of your head being chopped off."

Gabu began to cry.

"Don't waste time, Gabu. Rid the land of dust at once."

The king marched back to his palace.

"I must put my thinking cap on," said Gabu, and he put his head in his hands and began to think.

"When something is dirty, you brush it."

He asked all the villagers to help him. They took their brushes and brooms and ONE . . . TWO . . . THREE . . .

They all began to sweep – swish, swish, swish, swish, swish – all day long.

Until the dust rose up and filled the air in a thick, dark cloud. Everyone was coughing and spluttering and bumping into each other. The king choked, "Gabu, where are you? I asked you to rid the land of dust, not fill the air with dust. Gabu, you have two more days and ZUT!"

"Oh dear, oh dear," cried Gabu, and put his head in his hands and thought.

"When something is dirty, you wash it."

He asked all the villagers to help him. They took their buckets to the well and filled them up to the brims with water and

ONE . . . TWO . . . THREE . . .

They all began to pour – sloosh, sloosh, sloosh, sloosh, sloosh – all day long.

There was so much water it spread across the land. It began to rise. Soon it was up to their ankles, their knees, their waists and then up to their chests.

"Swim everybody," cried Gabu.

The king climbed to the top of the highest mountain where the water lapped his toes and he sniffed, "Gabu, a . . . atchoo! Where are you?"

Gabu came swimming.

"Yes, Your Majesty?"

"Gabu, I asked you to rid the land of dust not turn our village into a swimming pool. You have one more day and ZUT!"

"Oh dear, oh dear, I have run out of ideas," cried Gabu. The water trickled away and Gabu put his head in his hands and thought.

"I could put the king in an iron room with no windows or doors, chinks or cracks, then no speck of dust could creep in. But I don't think he would like that. Oh, if only

I could cover up all the dust with a carpet."
Then Gabu had a marvellous idea.

"Of course, why didn't I think of this before? Everyone has a needle and thread and a little piece of leather. Leather is tough, we will cover the land with leather."

He asked all the villagers to help him. Needles were threaded and knots were tied and ONE . . . TWO . . . THREE . . .

They all began to sew – stitch, stitch, stitch, stitch, stitch – all day long.

Then the huge piece of leather was spread across the land and it fitted perfectly. It stretched from the school to the well, from the temple to the palace, and all the way down to the river.

"We've done it," cried Gabu. "I will go and tell the king."

Gabu knocked on the palace door.

"We are ready, Your Majesty."

The king poked his head carefully around the door not knowing what to expect. Then a little smile twitched at the corners of his mouth. The ground looked clean, very clean indeed. He put one foot on the leather and it was spotless. The king walked across the leather.

"This is splendid, comfortable, clean. Well done, Gabu. Well done."

The king turned to the villagers to thank them.

Suddenly, out of the crowd stepped a little old man with a long white beard and a bent back. Everyone had quite forgotten him. He bowed low before the king and spoke in a very quiet voice.

"Your Majesty, how will anything be able to grow now that the land is covered with leather? The grass will not be able to push its way through. There will be no vegetables or flowers and no new trees. The animals will be hungry and there will be nothing for us to eat."

Now everyone was listening.

"Your Majesty, you know you don't have to cover the land with leather to keep your feet clean. It is really quite simple."

The old man took out of his pocket a large pair of scissors. He bent down and began to cut the leather carefully all around the king's feet. Then he took two laces from his pocket and tied each piece of leather to the king's feet. Then he pulled back the leather that covered the earth and said, "Try them, Your Majesty."

The king looked down at his feet covered in leather and frowned. He had never seen anything like it. He put one foot forward.

"Mmm, very good!" he exclaimed. He took another step.

"This is splendid, comfortable, clean *and* the grass can grow!"

Then the king walked, then he ran and then he jumped.

"Hooray," he cried. "I can walk here, and here, and here. I can walk anywhere and my feet will always be clean."

What was the king wearing on his feet?

That's right, he was wearing SHOES!

They were the first pair of shoes ever to be made, and people have been wearing them ever since.

SNIP, SNAP, SNOUT, MY STORY IS OUT!

A Surprise for Cyril!

SHOO RAYNER

Cyril was worried about Charlie. Charlie wasn't very well. He was getting fatter and fatter. He was getting slower and slower.

"Oh, Charlie," sighed Cyril, "I shall have to take you to the vet." He put the lock on the cat-flap so that Charlie couldn't get out of the house.

Whenever Charlie had to travel somewhere, Cyril would put him into a special basket that looked a bit like a cage. When Cyril brought it out from the cupboard under the stairs, Charlie would hear the basket creak and shoot off to find a good hiding-place. That's why Cyril locked the cat-flap first!

But this time, when Charlie heard the noise of the basket, he barely twitched his ears. He didn't even complain when Cyril put him in the basket, which he'd lined with fresh newspaper.

They looked at each other through the bars of the metal door. "Oh, Charlie," sighed Cyril again, "let's get going . . . see what the vet has to say about you."

"Well, Charlie," the vet said, in a business-like way, "let's see what the problem is." Then he felt Charlie's tummy. He prodded and poked, squidged and stroked and then he started to laugh! Cyril couldn't see what was funny.

"Well," said the vet, wiping a tear from the corner of his eye, "there's nothing to worry about. Charlie's quite well. In fact you will soon be surprised just how well he is!"

Then, still laughing, he gave Cyril some pills, which he said were vitamins that would help Charlie build his strength up.

When they got home Cyril tried to give Charlie his vitamins. He slipped one of the pills on to the back of Charlie's tongue. He held Charlie's mouth shut until he thought he had swallowed it. They looked at each other for a while then Cyril let go.

With a gentle cough the pill flew out of Charlie's mouth and shot across the kitchen floor.

Cyril tried again and again but Charlie would not swallow the pill. Then Cyril crushed it up and mixed it with Charlie's favourite food. But Charlie wasn't interested.

He sat by the cat-flap and waited for Cyril to unlock it, then he headed straight for the shed and squeezed into the space underneath. And there he stayed! He was still there when Cyril came to see him the next morning.

"I suppose he's all right," Cyril tut-tutted to himself. "The vet did say I'd be surprised how well he'd soon be. Perhaps he just needs to be left alone to rest." So that's what Cyril did. He left Charlie alone. He went shopping, then when he got back home, he made his lunch. He had just sat down to eat when he heard the sound of the cat-flap.

It was Charlie. He was carrying a tiny kitten in his mouth! He put the kitten into his basket and gave Cyril a big smile!

Cyril froze like a statue. His mouth was open and his fork-full of lunch stuck half-way between his plate and his mouth. Charlie went back through the cat-flap. He came back a minute later, with another kitten!

Charlie carried on, backwards and forwards, until there were four tiny kittens nuzzling up and drinking milk.

Cyril finally put his fork down and roared with laughter!

"The vet was right," he said, tickling Charlie between the ears. "You really have surprised me. All this time I thought you were a boy and now, here you are, a mummy with four dear little kittens of your own! They'll all need names, but first we'll have to think of a new name for you! Now . . . will it be Charlotte or Charlene?"

The Cock, the Mouse and the Little Red Hen

FÉLICITÉ LEFÈVRE

Once upon a time there was a hill, and on the hill there was a pretty little house.

It had one little green door, and four little windows with green shutters, and in it there lived A COCK, and A MOUSE, and A LITTLE RED HEN.

On another hill close by there was another little house. It was very ugly. It had a door that wouldn't shut, and two broken windows, and all the paint was off the shutters. And in this house there lived

A BOLD BAD FOX and FOUR BAD LITTLE FOXES.

One morning these four bad little foxes came to the big bad Fox, and said:

"Oh, Father, we're so hungry!"

"We had nothing to eat yesterday," said one.

"And scarcely anything the day before," said another.

"And only half a chicken the day before that," said the third.

"And only two little ducks the day before that," said the fourth.

The big bad Fox shook his head for a long time, for he was thinking. At last he said in a big gruff voice:

"On the hill over there I see a house. And in that house there lives a Cock."

"And a Mouse," screamed two of the little foxes.

"And a little Red Hen," screamed the other two.

"And they are nice and fat," went on the big bad Fox. "This very day, I'll take my great sack, and I will go up that hill, and in at that door, and into my sack I will put the Cock, and the Mouse, and the little Red Hen."

"I'll make a fire to roast the Cock," said one little fox.

"I'll put on the saucepan to boil the Hen," said the second.

"And I'll get the frying pan to fry the Mouse," said the third.

"And I'll have the biggest helping when they are all cooked," said the fourth, who was the greediest of all.

So the four little foxes jumped for joy, and the big bad Fox went to get his sack ready to start upon his journey.

But what was happening to the Cock and the Mouse, and the little Red Hen, all this time?

Well, sad to say, the Cock and the Mouse had both got out of bed on the wrong side that morning. The Cock said the day was too hot, and the Mouse grumbled because it was too cold.

They came grumbling down to the kitchen, where the good little Red Hen, looking as bright as a sunbeam, was bustling about.

"Who'll get some sticks to light the fire with?" she asked.

"*I* shan't," said the Cock.

"*I* shan't," said the Mouse.

"Then I'll do it myself," said the little Red Hen.

So off she ran to get the sticks.

"And now, who'll fill the kettle from the spring?" she asked.

"*I* shan't," said the Cock.

"*I* shan't," said the Mouse.

"Then I'll do it myself," said the little Red Hen.

And off she ran to fill the kettle.

"And who'll get the breakfast ready?" she asked, as she put the kettle on to boil.

"*I* shan't," said the Cock.

"*I* shan't," said the Mouse.

"Then I'll do it myself," said the little Red Hen.

All breakfast time the Cock and the Mouse quarrelled and grumbled. The Cock upset the milk jug, and the Mouse scattered crumbs upon the floor.

"Who'll clear away the breakfast?" asked the poor little Red Hen, hoping they would soon leave off being cross.

"*I* shan't," said the Cock.

"*I* shan't," said the Mouse.

"Then I'll do it myself," said the little Red Hen.

So she cleared everything away, swept up the crumbs and brushed up the fireplace.

"And now, who'll help me to make the beds?"

"*I* shan't," said the Cock.

"*I* shan't," said the Mouse.

"Then I'll do it myself," said the little Red Hen.

And she tripped away upstairs.

But the lazy Cock and Mouse each sat down in a comfortable armchair by the fire, and soon fell fast asleep.

Now the bad Fox had crept up the hill, and into the garden, and if the Cock and Mouse hadn't been asleep, they would have seen his sharp eyes peeping in at the window. "Rat tat tat, rat tat tat," the Fox knocked at the door.

"Who can that be?" said the Mouse, half opening his eyes.

"Go and look for yourself, if you want to know," said the rude Cock.

"It's the postman perhaps," thought the Mouse to himself, "and he may have a letter for me." So without waiting to see who it was, he lifted the latch and opened the door.

As soon as he opened it, in jumped the big Fox, with a cruel smile upon his face!

"Oh! oh! oh!" squeaked the Mouse, as he tried to run up the chimney.

"Doodle doodle do!" screamed the Cock, as he jumped on the back of the biggest armchair.

But the Fox only laughed, and without more ado he took the little Mouse by the tail and popped him into the sack, and seized the Cock by the neck and popped him in too.

Then the poor little Red Hen came running downstairs to see what all the noise was about, and the Fox caught her and put her into the sack with the others. Then he took a long piece of string out of his pocket, wound it round and round and round the mouth of the sack, and tied it very tightly indeed. After that he threw the sack over his back, and off he set down the hill.

"Oh! I wish I hadn't been so cross," said the Cock, as they went bumping about.

"Oh! I wish I hadn't been so lazy," said the Mouse, wiping his eyes with the tip of his tail.

"It's never too late to mend," said the little Red Hen, "and don't be too sad. See, here I have my little work-bag, and in it there is a pair of scissors, and a little thimble, and a needle and thread. Very soon you will see what I am going to do."

Now the sun was very hot, and soon Mr Fox began to feel his sack was heavy, and at last he thought he would lie down under a tree and go to sleep for a little while. So he threw the sack down with a big bump, and very soon fell fast asleep.

Snore, snore, snore, went the Fox.

As soon as the little Red Hen heard this, she took out her scissors, and began to snip a hole in the sack, just large enough for the Mouse to creep through.

"Quick," she whispered to the Mouse, "run as fast as you can and bring back a stone just as large as yourself."

Out scampered the Mouse, and soon came back, dragging the stone after him.

"Push it in here," said the little Red Hen, and he pushed it in in a twinkling.

Then the little Red Hen snipped away at the hole, till it was large enough for the Cock to get through.

"Quick," she said, "run and get a stone as big as yourself."

Out flew the Cock, and soon came back quite out of breath, with a big stone, which he pushed into the sack too.

Then the little Red Hen popped out, got a stone as big as herself, and pushed it in. Next she put on her thimble, took out her needle and thread, and sewed up the hole as quickly as ever she could.

When it was done, the Cock and the Mouse and the little Red Hen ran home very fast, shut the door after them, drew the bolts, shut the shutters, and drew down the blinds and felt quite safe.

The bad Fox lay fast asleep under the tree for some time, but at last he woke up.

"Dear, dear," he said, rubbing his eyes and then looking at the long shadows on the grass, "how late it is getting. I must hurry home."

So the bad Fox went grumbling and groaning down the hill, till he came to the stream. Splash! In went one foot. Splash! In went the other, but the stones in the sack were so heavy that at the very next step down tumbled Mr Fox into a deep pool. And then the fishes carried him off to their fairy caves and kept him a prisoner there, so he was never seen again. And the four greedy little foxes had to go to bed without any supper.

But the Cock and the Mouse never grumbled again. They lit the fire, filled the kettle, laid the breakfast, and did all the work, while the good little Red Hen had a holiday, and sat resting in the big armchair.

No foxes ever troubled them again, and for all I know they are still living happily in the little house with the green door and green shutters which stands on the hill.

Billy and the Best Umbrella

M. JOYCE DAVIES

"Billy," said Mother Bunny, "I want you to go to the village for me, to fetch a loaf, and some cakes, and a pound of sugar. *And* I want you to call at Great Aunt Rebecca's to fetch my umbrella that I left there yesterday. Take great care of the umbrella as you bring it home, because it is my very best new one. You'd better take your mackintosh with you," she added, "it looks as if it may rain."

So Billy put his mackintosh cape inside the shopping basket and set out for the village. When he got there he called first at Great Aunt Rebecca's house for his Mother's umbrella.

"Yes, to be sure!" said Great Aunt Rebecca, "she did leave it here yesterday." She gave Billy the new, neatly rolled umbrella. "Mind you are very careful of it," she said, "I'm sure your Mother would be vexed if any harm came to it."

Billy put the umbrella carefully under one arm, took his basket on the other arm, said "Goodbye" and "Thank you" to Great Aunt Rebecca, and went on to Mrs Badger's Baker's Shop.

Inside the shop he hung his mackintosh over his arm while Mrs Badger packed the bread, and cakes, and sugar into his basket for him. "There you are," she said kindly, "there's your shopping for you, and now you had best hurry home, I'm afraid it is going to rain. Still you'll be all right," she added, "I see you've got your mackintosh and umbrella with you."

"It isn't my umbrella," explained Billy,

"it's Mother's best new one, and I've got to take great care of it."

Billy set off towards home looking proudly at the new umbrella, but he had not gone far when he stopped, put down his basket, and held out a paw enquiringly.

Was it? Yes it was – a spot of rain! Two spots, three, four, five, six spots.

"Oh dear!" thought Billy in dismay. "What shall I do with Mother's best umbrella if it rains. It will *never* do to get it wet." He felt terribly worried for a minute or two, and then he suddenly had a brilliant idea. His mackintosh cape! Of course! If he wrapped his Mother's umbrella in the mackintosh it would keep beautifully dry.

He sighed with relief as he shook out the mackintosh, and then rolled the umbrella in it, taking great care to see that not even the tiniest scrap of umbrella was left uncovered. "That's all right now!" he said to himself, as he took up his shopping basket and started for home once more, hugging the well wrapped umbrella closely to him. It was raining faster now, and he hurried along as quickly as he could. "Oh dear!" he thought, "it is a pity I can't wear the mac, I *am* getting wet." He certainly was getting wet, wetter and wetter, and the rain came down faster and faster. He had to stop a minute every now and then to wrap the mackintosh more tightly round the umbrella, for he was determined not to let *that* get wet.

It seemed to him as if he would never reach home, but he struggled on until at last he stood drenched and dripping on his own doorstep.

Mother Bunny held up her hands in horror when she opened the door and saw her draggled little son.

"Billy!" she exclaimed. "Whatever *is* the matter? You're soaked through and through. Where's your mackintosh, and where's my umbrella?"

Triumphantly Billy unwrapped the wet bundle of mackintosh he was carrying. There inside was the best new umbrella, as dry as dry. "Here's your umbrella," he beamed, "and I *have* taken great care of it, Mother!"

Mother Bunny couldn't help laughing as he stood dripping all over her clean floor. "Oh, you silly, *silly* Billy," she cried, "the umbrella was meant to keep *you* dry. And oh, my poor cakes, and bread, and sugar – ruined!" she said, as she lifted a sodden pulpy mass out of the shopping basket.

"Oh!" gasped Billy in dismay, "I never even thought of the shopping, I was so worried about the best umbrella."

"Never mind," said his Mother as she rubbed him dry. "You did your best, and you certainly did take care of my umbrella."

She wrapped him in a blanket, sat him by a good fire, and gave him a bowl of hot soup to drink so that he shouldn't catch cold.

The Sweet Porridge

WANDA GÁG

Once there was a poor but worthy girl who lived with her mother in a little village. They were so poor, these two, that many a night they had to go hungry to bed, and at last there came a time when there was nothing left in the house for them to eat. Now the girl, hoping perhaps to find some nuts or berries, went out into the woods, where she met an old woman. Strangely enough, the woman already knew that the two were in trouble and, handing the girl a little cooking kettle, she said, "Take this, my child. If you set it on the stove and say to it 'Cook, little kettle, cook,' it will start bubbling and boiling and will cook up a mess of good, sweet millet porridge for you and your mother. Then, when you have eaten your fill, you need only to say, 'Stop, little kettle, stop,' and it will stop cooking until the next time."

And that was the way it turned out to be. The girl took the kettle home to her mother, and now the two could eat all the sweet porridge they wanted and were never hungry any more.

One day the girl went away for a few hours and the mother, feeling hungry, said, "Cook, little kettle, cook." Immediately a good hearty smell filled the kitchen, the kettle began to cook, and soon the mother was enjoying a big bowl of good, sweet porridge. But when she had eaten her fill and wanted to make the kettle stop cooking, she found she had forgotten the right words.

So the little kettle kept on cooking – cooked and cooked until the porridge rose over the rim of the kettle. Cooked and cooked some more until it flowed all over the stove. Cooked and cooked and kept on cooking until the little cottage was filled with porridge. Cooked and cooked until it poured out of the windows into the street, and then into all the huts and cottages along the way.

At this the people ran from their houses to escape from the bubbling, boiling flood, but the porridge cooked merrily on until it had filled the whole village. Even then it didn't stop but spread out over the fields, flowing in all directions as though it were trying to feed the whole world. Everyone was worried, but no one knew what to do.

At last, when only one little hut was left unfilled with porridge, the girl returned. When she saw what had happened, she quickly cried, "Stop, little kettle, stop!" And of course the kettle obeyed and stopped cooking – but the only way the village folk could return to their houses was to eat their way through the porridge!

Hedgehogs Don't Eat Hamburgers

VIVIAN FRENCH

Hector saw a picture on a paper bag.

"What's that?" he asked.

"That's a hamburger," said his dad.

"Can I have one for my tea?" asked Hector.

"No," said his dad. "Hedgehogs don't eat hamburgers."

"I do," said Hector. "And I'm going to go and find one for my tea."

Hector set off to find a hamburger.

"Here I go, here I go, here I go," he sang as he walked along.

Hattie popped out to see who was going by.

"Hello," said Hector. "I'm going to find my tea."

"Would you like some fine fat snails?" Hattie asked.

"No thank you," said Hector. "I'm going to find a hamburger."

"Hedgehogs don't eat hamburgers," said Hattie.

"I do," said Hector.

"Oh," said Hattie. "Maybe I'll come too."

So she did.

Hector and Hattie set off to find a hamburger.

"Here we go, here we go, here we go," they sang as they walked along.

Harry popped out to see who was going by.

"Hello," said Hector. "We're going to find my tea."

"Would you like some slow slimy slugs?" Harry asked. "I've got plenty."

"No thank you," said Hector. "I'm going to find a hamburger."

"Hedgehogs don't eat hamburgers," said Harry.

"I do," said Hector.

"Oh," said Harry. "Maybe I'll come too."

So he did.

Hector and Hattie and Harry set off to find a hamburger.

"Here we go, here we go, here we go," they sang as they walked along.

Hester popped out to see who was going by.

"Hello," said Hector. "We're going to find my tea."

"Would you like some big black beetles?" Hester asked. "I've got lots."

"No thank you," said Hector. "I'm going to find a hamburger."

"Hedgehogs don't eat hamburgers," said Hester.

"I do," said Hector.

"Oh," said Hester. "Maybe I'll come too."

So she did.

Hector and Hattie and Harry and Hester set off to find a hamburger.

"Here we go, here we go, here we go," they sang as they walked along.

Fox popped out to see who was going by.

"Hello," said Hector. "We're going to find my tea."

"Tea, eh?" said Fox. "What a good idea." He looked at the fat little hedgehogs, and he licked his lips.

"I'm going to find a hamburger," said Hector.

"WHAT a good idea," said Fox. "Shall I show you the way?"

"YES, PLEASE," said Hector.

Hector and Hattie and Harry and Hester set off after Fox.

"Here we go, here we go, here we go," they sang as they walked along.

"SSSHHH!" said Fox.

"Oh," said Hector and Hattie and Harry and Hester.

They walked up the hill and down the hill.

"Are we nearly there?" asked Hector.

"Nearly," said Fox. He sniffed the air. "Yes, we're nearly there."

Hector sniffed the air too. "What is it?" he asked.

"That's the smell of the town," said Fox. "That's where the hamburgers are."

"Oh," said Hector. He sniffed the air again. He could smell cars, and smoke, and shops, and houses. He could smell danger. "Maybe I don't want a hamburger today. Maybe I'll have big black beetles, or slow slimy slugs, or fine fat snails. Maybe hedgehogs don't eat hamburgers after all."

Hector turned round, and Hattie and Harry and Hester all turned round too.

"Here we go, here we go, here we go!" they sang.

"JUST A MINUTE," said Fox, and he opened his mouth wide. His teeth were sharp and white. "What about MY tea?"

"YOU can have a hamburger," said Hector.

"But I don't WANT a hamburger," said Fox. "I want little fat HEDGEHOGS!"

And he jumped at Hector and Hattie and Harry and Hester.

"HERE WE GO, HERE WE GO, HERE WE GO," sang all four little hedgehogs, and they rolled themselves up tightly into four prickly balls.

"OWWWW!" said Fox as he hurt his nose. "OW! OW! OW!" He turned round and ran up the hill and down the hill. He didn't stop running until he got home to his mummy.

Hector and Hattie and Harry and Hester looked at each other.

"Let's go home," said Hector.

So they all set off to go home.

"Home we go, home we go, home we go," they sang as they walked up the hill and down the hill. And they got home just in time to have fine fat snails, slow slimy slugs and big black beetles for their tea.

The Pudding Like a Night on the Sea

ANN CAMERON

"I'm going to make something special for your mother," my father said.

My mother was out shopping. My father was in the kitchen looking at the pots and the pans and the jars of this and that.

"What are you going to make?" I said.

"A pudding," he said.

My father is a big man with wild black hair. When he laughs, the sun laughs in the windowpanes. When he thinks, you can almost see his thoughts sitting on all the tables and chairs. When he is angry, my little brother, Huey, and I shiver to the bottom of our shoes.

"What kind of pudding will you make?" Huey said.

"A wonderful pudding," my father said. "It will taste like a whole raft of lemons. It will taste like a night on the sea."

Then he took down a knife and sliced five lemons in half. He squeezed the first one. Juice squirted in my eye.

"Stand back!" he said, and squeezed again. The seeds flew out on the floor. "Pick up those seeds, Huey," he said.

Huey took the broom and swept them up.

My father cracked some eggs and put the yolks in a pan and the whites in a bowl. He rolled up his sleeves and pushed back his hair and beat up the yolks.

"Sugar, Julian!" he said, and I poured in the sugar.

He went on beating. Then he put in lemon juice and cream and set the pan on the stove. The pudding bubbled and he stirred it fast. Cream splashed on the stove.

"Wipe that up, Huey!" he said.

Huey did.

It was hot by the stove. My father loosened his collar and pushed at his sleeves. The stuff in the pan was getting thicker and thicker. He held the beater up high in the air. "Just right!" he said, and sniffed in the smell of the pudding.

He whipped the egg whites and mixed them into the pudding. The pudding looked softer and lighter than air.

"Done!" he said. He washed all the pots, splashing water on the floor, and wiped the counter so fast his hair made circles around his head.

"Perfect!" he said. "Now I'm going to take a nap. If something important happens, bother me. If nothing important happens, don't bother me. And – the pudding is for your mother. Leave the pudding alone!"

He went to the living room and was asleep in a minute, sitting straight up in his chair.

Huey and I guarded the pudding.

"Oh, it's a wonderful pudding," Huey said.

"With waves on the top like the ocean," I said.

"I wonder how it tastes," Huey said.

"Leave the pudding alone," I said.

"If I just put my finger in – there – I'll know how it tastes," Huey said.

And he did it.

"You did it!" I said. "How does it taste?"

"It tastes like a whole raft of lemons," he said. "It tastes like a night on the sea."

"You've made a hole in the pudding!" I said. "But since you did it, I'll have a taste." And it tasted like a whole night of lemons. It tasted like floating at sea.

"It's such a big pudding," Huey said. "It can't hurt to have a little more."

"Since you took more, I'll have more," I said.

"That was a bigger lick than I took!" Huey said. "I'm going to have more again."

"Whoops!" I said.

"You put in your whole hand!" Huey said. "Look at the pudding you spilled on the floor!"

"I am going to clean it up," I said. And I took the rag from the sink.

"That's not really clean," Huey said.

"It's the best I can do," I said.

"Look at the pudding!" Huey said.

It looked like craters on the moon. "We have to smooth this over," I said. "So it looks the way it did before! Let's get spoons."

And we evened the top of the pudding with spoons, and while we evened it, we ate some more.

"There isn't much left," I said.

"We were supposed to leave the pudding alone," Huey said.

"We'd better get away from here," I said. We ran into our bedroom and crawled under the bed. After a long time we heard my father's voice.

"Come into the kitchen, dear," he said. "I have something for you."

"Why, what is it?" my mother said, out in the kitchen.

Under the bed, Huey and I pressed ourselves to the wall.

"Look," said my father, out in the kitchen. "A wonderful pudding."

"Where is the pudding?" my mother said.

"WHERE ARE YOU BOYS?" my father said. His voice went through every crack and corner of the house.

We felt like two leaves in a storm.

"WHERE ARE YOU? I SAID!" My father's voice was booming.

Huey whispered to me, "I'm scared."

We heard my father walking slowly through the rooms.

"Huey!" he called. "Julian!" We could see his feet. He was coming into our room.

He lifted the bedspread. There was his face, and his eyes like black lightning. He grabbed us by the legs and pulled. "STAND UP!" he said.

We stood.

"What do you have to tell me?" he said.

"We went outside," Huey said, "and when we came back, the pudding was gone!"

"Then why were you hiding under the bed?" my father said.

We didn't say anything. We looked at the floor.

"I can tell you one thing," he said. "There is going to be some beating here now! There is going to be some whipping!"

The curtains at the window were shaking. Huey was holding my hand.

"Go into the kitchen!" my father said. "Right now!"

We went to the kitchen.

"Come here, Huey!" my father said.

Huey walked towards him, his hands behind his back.

"See these eggs?" my father said. He cracked them and put the yolks in a pan and set the pan on the counter. He stood a chair by the counter. "Stand up here," he said to Huey.

Huey stood on the chair by the counter.

"Now it's time for your beating!" my father said.

Huey started to cry. His tears fell in with the egg yolks.

"Take this!" my father said. My father handed him the egg beater. "Now beat those eggs," he said. "I want this to be a good beating!"

"Oh!" Huey said. He stopped crying. And he beat the egg yolks.

"Now you, Julian, stand here!" my father said.

I stood on a chair by the table.

"I hope you're ready for your whipping!"

I didn't answer. I was afraid to say yes or no.

"Here!" he said, and he set the egg whites in front of me. "I want these whipped and whipped well!"

"Yes, sir!" I said, and started whipping.

My father watched us. My mother came into the kitchen and watched us.

After a while Huey said, "This is hard work."

"That's too bad," my father said. "Your beating's not done!" And he added sugar and cream and lemon juice to Huey's pan and put the pan on the stove. And Huey went on beating.

"My arm hurts from whipping," I said.

"That's too bad," my father said. "Your whipping's not done."

So I whipped and whipped, and Huey beat and beat.

"Hold that beater in the air, Huey!" my father said.

Huey held it in the air. "See!" my father said. "A good pudding stays on the beater. It's thick enough now. Your beating's done." Then he turned to me. "Let's see those egg whites, Julian!" he said. They were puffed up and fluffy. "Congratulations, Julian!" he said. "Your whipping's done."

He mixed the egg whites into the pudding himself. Then he passed the pudding to my mother.

"A wonderful pudding," she said. "Would you like some, boys?"

"No thank you," we said.

She picked up a spoon. "Why, this tastes like a whole raft of lemons," she said. "This tastes like a night on the sea."

The Horrendous Hullabaloo

MARGARET MAHY

There was once a cheerful old woman who kept house for her nephew, Peregrine – a pirate by profession.

Every morning she put on her pirate pinafore, poured out Peregrine's ration of rum, picked up his socks, and petted his parrot. She worked day in, day out, keeping everything shipshape.

Meanwhile, her pirate nephew went out to parties every night, though he never once asked his aunt or his parrot if they would like to go with him.

Whenever his aunt suggested that she and the parrot might want to come too, Peregrine replied, "You wouldn't enjoy pirate parties, dear aunt. The hullabaloo is horrendous!"

"But I like horrendous hullabaloos!" exclaimed the aunt. "And so does the parrot."

"When I come back from sea I want a break from the parrot," said Peregrine, looking proud and piratical. "And if I took my aunt to a party, all the other pirates would laugh at me."

"Very well," thought his aunt, "I shall have a party of my own."

Without further ado she sent out masses of invitations written in gold ink. Then she baked batch after batch of delicious rumble-bumpkins while the parrot hung upside down on a pot plant, clacking its beak greedily.

No sooner had Peregrine set off that evening on another night's hullabaloo than his aunt, shutting the door behind him, peeled off her pirate pinafore and put on her patchwork party dress.

"Half-past seven!" she called to the parrot. "We'll soon be having a horrendous hullabaloo of our own!"

Then she opened the windows and sat waiting for the guests to come, enjoying the salty scent of the sea, and the sound of waves washing around Peregrine's pirate ship, out in the moonlit bay.

"Half-past eight!" chimed the clock. The pirate's aunt waited.

"Half-past nine!" chimed the clock. The pirate's aunt still waited, shuffling her feet and tapping her fingers.

"Half-past ten!" chimed the clock. The rumblebumpkins were in danger of burning. No one, it seemed, was brave enough to come to a party at a pirate's house. The pirate's aunt shed bitter tears over the rumblebumpkins.

Suddenly the parrot spoke. "I have lots of friends who love rumblebumpkins," she cackled. "Friends who aren't put in a panic or petrified by pirates – friends who would happily help with a hullabaloo!"

"Well, what are you waiting for?" cried

the pirate's aunt. "Go and fetch them at once!"

Out of the window the parrot flew, while the aunt mopped up her tears and patted powder on her nose.

Almost at once the night air was filled with flapping and fluttering. The sea swished and sighed. The night breeze smelled of passion-fruit, pineapples and palm trees. In through the open windows tumbled the patchwork party guests, all screeching with laughter. They were speckled, they were freckled; they were streaked and striped like the rollicking rags of rainbow. All the parrots in town had come to the aunt's party.

"Come one, come all!" the aunt cried happily.

The parrots cackled loudly, breaking into a bit of a sing-song. So loud was the sing-song that the pirate's neighbours all rushed out of their houses, prepared for the worst.

"What a horrendous hullabaloo!" they cried in amazement.

The aunt invited them all to feast richly on her rumblebumpkins, and to join her in a wild jig. She was having a wonderful time.

When Peregrine arrived home later that night, his house was still ringing with left-over echoes of a horrendous hullabaloo. The air smelled strongly of rumblebumpkins, and the floor was covered with parrot feathers.

"Aunt!" he called crossly. "Come and tidy up at once."

But there was no one at home for, at that very moment, his aunt, still wearing her patchwork party dress, was stealing away on Peregrine's own pirate ship.

Over the moonlit sea she was sailing, with parrots perched all over her, making a horrendous hullabaloo. As they sailed off in search of passion-fruit, pineapples and palm trees, it was impossible to tell where the aunt left off and the parrots began.

So left on his own, with a grunt and a groan, Peregrine put on the pirate pinafore and tidied up for himself.

New Blue Shoes

EVE RICE

One afternoon, Mama walked into the living room holding Rebecca's coat.

"Put away your crayons," Mama said. "We are going shopping."

Rebecca was just finishing a drawing of a man fishing.

"Do you like it?" she asked.

"Yes, it is beautiful," said Mama, "but we are going shopping. Put your crayons away."

Rebecca put all the crayons in their box. Then she put on her grey coat.

"Are you ready?" Mama asked.

"Ready," said Rebecca.

They walked into town.

Mama stopped in front of a shoe shop and opened the door.

"We have to buy a new pair of shoes," she said.

"For you?" asked Rebecca.

"No," said Mama, "for you."

Mama walked into the shop and sat down. Rebecca sat down beside her. Then they waited.

Finally a salesman came over.

"We would like some shoes," said Mama.

The salesman measured Rebecca's feet.

"Size nine," he said. "What colour would you like?"

"Blue," Rebecca said before her mother could answer.

"Blue?" said Mama. "I think brown would be much nicer. Brown."

"Blue," said Rebecca. "I want blue."

"All right, blue," said Mama.

"I'll see what we have," said the salesman.

The salesman took down boxes and boxes of brand-new shoes – with buckles and bows and little black buttons. Then he came back. He held up one pair after another.

"No," Rebecca said, "I want *nice* shoes. I want new blue, nice blue, nice new blue shoes!"

"Shhh," said Mama. "Don't make the nice man angry." Mama turned to the salesman.

"Don't you have any plain blue shoes?"

The salesman went into the back of the shop. He took down boxes and more boxes. And in the very last box on the very last shelf, he found a pair of plain blue shoes. The salesman brought out the shoes for Rebecca and her mother to see. Then he fitted the shoes on Rebecca's feet. They were very nice blue shoes.

Rebecca got up, walked in two big circles, and stopped in front of the mirror.

"OK?" Mama asked.

"OK."

"We'll take them," said Mama.

The salesman took off Rebecca's new shoes and put them in a box.

Mama paid for the shoes.

Then Mama and Rebecca started home.

Along the way, Rebecca stopped.

"What's the matter?" Mama asked.

"I think my feet will look silly in blue shoes," said Rebecca. "Maybe we should get a different pair of shoes. Maybe we should get brown shoes."

"Or maybe we should get a different pair of feet," Mama said. "Do you suppose there is a store nearby that sells new feet?"

"No," said Rebecca. "No. I like my very own feet."

"Well, I like the shoes," Mama said, "and I think your feet will look just fine in blue shoes."

Rebecca thought for a minute. "Maybe."

"Come along," said Mama.

Rebecca and her mother walked home.

"Put on your new shoes and wear them around the house," Mama said as she took out her crocheting and sat down.

Rebecca took her new shoes out of their box and put them on. Then she brought out her crayons and drew a picture of a lady with a dog.

"Look, Mama."

"It's splendid," said Mama, "just splendid."

"Mama?" said Rebecca.

"Yes?"

"Blue shoes don't look silly on my feet at all. I like them."

"That's nice," said Mama. "I'm glad you like your new shoes. Blue is such a splendid colour."

"Mama?"

"Yes, Rebecca?"

"You can't *really* buy new feet. That's just silly – isn't it?"

"I guess so," Mama said.

"I like my feet the way they are," said Rebecca.

"So do I," said Mama. "As a matter of fact, I like all of you the way you are – right down to your very own feet in your new blue shoes."

The Magic Scissors

LOES SPAANDER

Once upon a time, far, far away in a half-forgotten part of the world, between high mountains and a deep, blue lake, there was a little Chinese boy and his name was Liu Chu.

He lived with his father and mother in a little bamboo hut and he was very happy. All day long he played in the sand or he sat in the sun and looked at the birds and the flowers. And when he was hungry his mother gave him a bowl of rice, and he ate it with his fingers, and nobody minded.

One day his mother said to him: "Liu Chu, there is not enough rice today. Go to the lake and catch some fish for dinner."

Liu Chu, who was a good little boy, went to the back of the hut to fetch his fishnet. Then he trotted off to the lake.

It was a long way and the day was very hot. But Liu Chu was used to the sun and did not mind a bit. He whistled as he went and soon reached the lake. There he threw his net into the water and caught a beautiful, big red-and-blue-and-silver fish. Liu Chu was very glad, but the red-and-blue-and-silver fish said: "Dear Liu Chu, please, please, let me go and I promise you a wonderful pair of magic scissors; whatever you cut out with them will come to life."

So Liu Chu let the red-and-blue-and-silver fish go and found himself holding a wonderful pair of scissors instead.

Liu Chu was delighted. He took a scrap of golden paper and cut a beautiful little castle. No sooner was it ready than it grew and grew, and to his surprise the little boy saw an immense golden castle arising before him.

Then Liu Chu thought of the lovely garden that should surround it, and with the scissors he cut out tree after tree, flower after flower, the one more beautiful than the other, and they all grew and became real. And he also cut out pretty little birds that filled the air with their sweet music.

Liu Chu then ran home to fetch his parents. But when he saw them in their ragged old clothes, he decided to make them new ones first.

He set to work with his scissors, and the little paper garments he made became magnificent clothes of silk and brocade. Soon they all were dressed in them and Liu Chu led the way to the castle.

His parents were full of admiration and wonder and went to look inside. Liu Chu, left alone in the garden, decided to make himself some little playmates. He cut some paper dolls. They fluttered around him and became lifelike, and in no time a whole swarm of cheerful little boys and girls were dancing around him, crying happily, "Liu Chu, be our friend, come and play with us."

Thus Liu Chu made everything under the sun that should fill a little boy with happiness. The castle became their new home. There were so many rooms that nobody had ever seen them all, and each one was furnished in grand style and with exquisite taste. There were the most precious toys and delightful books, but yet, the more he had the unhappier he became. One by one his old pleasures were taken away from him.

If he ate with his fingers his father would box his ears and say: "What are your chopsticks for, young rascal!"

And if he played in the sand, his mother would scold and say: "Liu Chu dear, think of your beautiful new clothes, you'll spoil them."

Worst of all there was no more time to play. All day long from breakfast to supper-time there were lessons to study. Learned professors came to teach Liu Chu reading and writing and arithmetic, geography, history and oh! so many other things. Liu Chu was sure he never would remember all he had to learn.

Outside he could hear the happy cries of his little playmates and he would think of the old days, when he, too, was out in the sun, laughing and playing, watching the birds and the flowers.

So, day by day, little Liu Chu grew less happy. One night he could not sleep, but lay tossing about in his bed. At last he got up and softly went out of his bedroom.

He tiptoed through the sleeping palace and silent gardens and ventured out of the gate.

The moon was shining very brightly, making a magic world out of the one Liu Chu knew so well. He shivered a little with the cold of the night, but he went on bravely to find his way to the lake. There he looked for his friend, the red-and-blue-and-silver fish.

"Fish," he cried, "red-and-blue-and-silver fish, it's me, Liu Chu. I am no longer happy. Can't you help me?"

The fish peeped out of the water. "Little friend," he said, "you have grown too rich, and wealth does not always mean happiness; take your scissors, and at sunrise whistle thrice and throw them into the lake. Then you will be rich no more, but you may be happy again."

The fish disappeared and Liu Chu sat down to wait for the sun to come up. At last, the pale dawn crept slowly over the mountains, and soon the earth was filled with light and warmth. Liu Chu threw away his scissors into the lake and went home hopefully.

There he found the old bamboo hut again. His mother in her old clothes was waiting for him with a bowl of rice. She smiled at him. And Liu Chu, sitting down on the warm, yellow sand to gobble up his rice, felt that once more he was the happiest boy in the world.

Learning to Swim

STAN CULLIMORE

"Henrietta. Wakey, wakey, or we will be late." Henrietta's mother put down the tray of green bananas she was carrying and opened the curtains in Henrietta's room. Henrietta opened one eye.

"Late for what?"

"You haven't forgotten what day it is, have you?" said her mother. "Today is Saturday." Henrietta pulled a face.

"Ratburgers," she groaned as she sat up in bed. "I hate Saturdays."

Up until the last two weeks, Henrietta

had loved Saturdays. But now she had changed her mind. Saturday was the day when all the family went to the swimming pool and Henrietta had her swimming lesson.

"Boring," grumped Henrietta as she ate her green bananas in bed. "I hate water and I don't want to learn to swim." As her mother turned to leave the room Henrietta put her banana skin under the pillow and folded her arms.

Her mother sighed.

"Daniel can swim."

Henrietta snorted. "He's a show-off." Her mother sighed once more.

"Daniel isn't a show-off. He is just a good swimmer. You could be a good swimmer, young lady, if you just tried a little bit harder at your swimming lessons. And stopped acting like such a baby."

She went off to make breakfast for Baby-Rose and Dad.

Henrietta lay in bed and looked at the ceiling.

"It's not fair."

Suddenly she jumped up and began to dance around the room. "What a brilliant idea," she cried. "No more swimming lessons for me. I've got a secret plan. Yippee!"

She picked up her felt-tip pens and her box of blue balloons. Then she skipped into the kitchen.

After breakfast the whole family set off for the swimming pool. Henrietta, her mother and her father pushing Baby-Rose in the buggy. Her sensible brother Daniel was carrying the towels.

"How come Henrietta never carries anything?" asked Daniel. "I'm always the helpful one."

"What a creep," muttered Henrietta. She was never helpful.

Usually, when they walked to the swimming pool, Henrietta stayed at the back . . . holding a tickling stick. And sometimes, only sometimes, it would ever so accidentally tickle Daniel's legs as he walked.

"Stop it, Henrietta," Daniel would say. "Stop it or I'll tell."

"Oh sorry, Daniel," Henrietta would reply. Then the tickling stick would accidentally tickle Daniel again.

But today Henrietta ran along in front holding on to her felt-tip pens.

"Now where did I put my balloons? Ah, here they are." She had hidden them in one of her pockets.

When she got to the swimming pool Henrietta looked around her. The others hadn't finished changing yet.

"Better make sure that no one can see me," she thought. Quickly she blew up a balloon and using her felt-tip pen she drew on it a pair of eyes, just like her own eyes. Then a nose, just like her own nose.

Then she placed the balloon in the swimming pool and pushed it, so that it floated right out into the middle of the deep end. She sniggered to herself and hid behind a chair.

Soon the rest of the family arrived.

"Look," cried Mum, pointing at the balloon. "What on earth is that?"

Henrietta's father gasped and started to laugh. Then he nudged Daniel and winked at Mum.

"Good grief," he said, "I think it's Henrietta. Doesn't she look strange. Her face has gone blue!" Behind the chair Henrietta sniggered and snorted.

"My plan is working. No more stupid swimming lessons for me." Her father picked up Baby-Rose and pointed at the balloon.

"Look at your big sister. Isn't she clever learning to swim all by herself." Behind the chair Henrietta was having to hold her nose to stop herself from laughing.

"Yes I am clever," she chuckled, "and so is my plan." She scratched her nose.

Her mother waved at the balloon.

"Henrietta," she laughed, "you are a clever little girl. I told you that you could be a good swimmer if you tried." But Henrietta did not hear them all laughing at the balloon, she was too busy laughing herself.

"They think I'm in the water," she snorted, "but I'm not."

By now she was laughing so hard that she could not stand up.

"Hehehe," she laughed. "Hohoho."

She noticed her nose was feeling all tickly. "That's funny," she laughed. "It feels as if someone is tickling my nose with a tickling stick, ah . . . tickling stick, ah . . . Oh no, not my sneezy nose." She tried to hold it with both hands. But it was too late.

"Atishoo." She did a Henrietta hyper-sneeze that blew her over the chair and into the swimming pool. Right on top of the balloon.

When she opened her eyes Henrietta saw her mother and father and even Baby-Rose all staring at her.

"Hahaha. Fooled you," cried Henrietta. "You thought that silly balloon was me. Well it wasn't. I was hiding behind the chair all the time."

Then she saw her sensible brother Daniel.

He was standing behind the chair, holding the biggest, tickliest tickling stick Henrietta had ever seen.

"You knew all along," cried Henrietta. "it was you tickling my nose, wasn't it. You made me sneeze and fall into the water. And I can't even swim. HELP." Just then Henrietta noticed something.

"I'm swimming. Mum, Dad, look."

"I told you that if you tried you could swim, Henrietta." But Henrietta did not hear her. She was too busy sticking out her tongue at Daniel.

Mashenka and the Bear

A Russian Story

JAMES RIORDAN

An old peasant and his wife had a granddaughter, Mashenka. One summer's day, the little girl's friends called on her to go mushrooming with them in the meadow.

"Granny, Grandad," cried Mashenka. "May I go out to play? I'll bring you lots of mushrooms, I promise."

"Run along then," the old pair said, "but mind you don't go near the forest or else the wolves or bears will get you."

Off skipped the girls towards the

meadow at the forest edge. Mashenka knew that the best and biggest mushrooms grew beneath the trees and bushes in the forest. Almost without noticing it, she wandered out of sight of her friends. She moved from tree to tree, from bush to bush, picking a basketful of mushrooms – reds and yellows, browns and whites. All the while she went deeper and deeper into the forest. Suddenly, she looked up and realized she was lost.

"Hell-oooo! Hell-oooo!" she called.

There was no reply.

Someone heard her none the less.

From the trees came a rustling and a cracking, and out stepped a big brown bear. When he set eyes on the little girl, he threw up his arms in joy.

"Aha!" he cried. "You'll make a fine servant for me, my pretty one."

Taking the girl roughly by the arm, he dragged her to his cottage in the depths of the dark wood. Once inside, he growled at her, "Now stoke the fire, cook some porridge and make my home clean and tidy."

There now began a miserable life in the bear's cottage for poor Mashenka. Day after day she toiled from dawn to dusk, afraid the bear would eat her. All the while she thought of how she could escape. Finally, an idea came to her.

"Mister Bear," she said politely, "may I go home for a day to show my grandparents I am alive and well?"

"Certainly not," growled the bear. "You'll never leave here. If you have a message I'll take it myself."

That was just what Mashenka had planned. She baked some cherry pies, piled them on a dish and fetched a big basket. Then she called the bear.

"Mister Bear, I'll put the pies in this basket for you to carry home. Remember, though, not to open the basket and don't touch the pies. I'll be watching. When you set off I'll climb on to the roof to keep an eye on you."

"All right, pretty one," grumbled the bear. "Just let me take a nap before I go."

No sooner was thc bear asleep than

Mashenka quickly climbed on to the roof and made a lifelike figure out of a pole, her coat and headscarf. Then she scrambled down, squeezed into the basket and pulled the dish of cherry pies over her head. When the bear woke up and saw the basket ready, he hoisted it on to his broad back and set off for the village.

Through the trees he ambled with his load and soon he felt tired and footsore. Stopping by a tree stump, he sank down to rest, thinking of eating a cherry pie. But just as he was about to open the basket, he heard Mashenka's voice.

"Don't sit there all day and don't you touch those pies."

Glancing round he could just see her figure on his roof.

"My, my, that maid has sharp eyes," he mumbled to himself.

Up he got and continued on his way.

On and on he went, carrying the heavy load.

Soon he came upon another tree stump.

"I'll just take a rest and eat a cherry

pie," he thought, puffing and panting. Yet once again Mashenka's muffled voice was heard.

"Don't sit down and don't touch those pies. Go straight to the village as I told you."

He looked back but could no longer see his house.

"Well, I'll be jiggered!" he exclaimed. "She's got eyes like a hawk, that girl."

So on he went.

Through the trees he shuffled, down into the valley, on through groves of ash, up grassy knolls until, finally, he emerged into a meadow.

"I must rest my poor feet," he sighed. "And I'll just have one small pie to refresh me. She surely cannot see me now."

But from out of nowhere came a distant voice.

"I can see you! I can see you! Don't you touch those cherry pies! Go on, Mister Bear."

The bear was puzzled, even scared.

"What an extraordinary girl she is,"

he growled, hurrying across the field.

At last he arrived at the village, stopped at Mashenka's door and knocked loudly.

"Open up, open up!" he cried gruffly. "I've brought a present from your granddaughter."

The moment they heard his voice, however, dogs came running from all the yards. Their barking startled him so much, he left the basket at the door and made off towards the forest without a backward glance.

How surprised Mashenka's grandparents were when they opened the door, found the basket and saw no one in sight.

Grandad lifted up the lid, stared hard and could scarcely believe his eyes. For there beneath the cherry pies sat the little girl, alive and well.

Granny and Grandad both danced with joy, hugged Mashenka and said what a clever girl she was to trick the bear. Soon all her friends heard the news and came running to hug and kiss her too. Mashenka was so happy.

In the meantime, deep in the forest, the old bear had reached home and shouted to the figure on the roof to make his tea. Of course, it did not take him long to learn that the wise young girl had tricked him.

Ian's Useful Collection

MARGARET JOY

Miss Mee taught the youngest children at Allotment Lane School. There were about twenty children in her class and one of them was a boy called Ian. Now Ian was most particular about his trousers and *always* had pockets in them. Whenever he had new trousers he always said, "I don't mind if they're short trousers to my knees or long trousers to my ankles. I don't mind if they're red or green or brown. But they *must* have pockets."

The boy's name was Ian. And can you

guess why Ian had to have pockets? It was to keep things in, of course. But he didn't just keep a clean hanky in them – oh, no!

Ian was a collector, just like the rest of his family. His father collected screws and nails. If he saw any curly screws or sharp nails lying about, he would pick them up and look at them and say, "They might just come in useful." Then he would keep them in his tool box.

Ian's mother was a collector too. She collected clean paper bags. Whenever she brought shopping home, she would take the things out of their paper bags and say, "What lovely clean paper bags. They might just come in useful." Then she would smooth them out and put them on top of all the other clean paper bags in the kitchen drawer.

Ian's big sister was another collector. She collected pictures of pop stars and stuck them all over the walls of her bedroom. Whenever she saw a picture or poster in a magazine, she would say, "Cor, that's a great picture. That'll just do for my collection." Then she would run upstairs and try to find a space for it on her bedroom wall.

Ian didn't collect screws or nails, *or* paper bags, *or* pictures of pop stars. He collected anything at all that was interesting and fitted into his trouser pockets. When he was very, very little he once collected a pocketful of snow! You can guess what happened to that, can't you?

One morning Ian set out for school. He had clean trousers on, so his pockets were quite empty. He walked along, as he usually did, with his head bent so that he could look for interesting things on the ground as he walked along.

The first thing he spotted was a strong, thick rubber band. He knew who dropped rubber bands – the post woman! She often walked along the road with a bundle of letters, and Ian had seen her slip the rubber band off the bundle and drop it on the path. He picked it up and put it in his pocket.

Next he saw a very flat, round pebble.

It was like the pebbles Ian had seen on the beach at the seaside. It was lovely to hold, cool and smooth, and Ian put it in his other pocket.

He walked a little further, still looking. Then he noticed a silver safety pin. It was shining in the sunshine and wasn't at all dirty or rusty, so Ian picked it up and put it in the pocket with the rubber band.

The next thing his sharp eyes noticed was a matchbox. It was quite clean and new. Ian opened it and sniffed. It smelt just like matches: a funny smell that made his nose wrinkle. He was very pleased with the empty matchbox, and he put it into the pocket with the rubber band and the safety pin.

He nearly missed seeing a long piece of green string near the hedge. He picked it up and rolled it round his fingers and put it in the pocket with the smooth, cool pebble. Now he was nearly at the school gate. He began to jog along, kicking a tiny broken piece of red brick in front of him. Then he thought, "I suppose that might come in useful too." So he picked it up and put it in the pocket with the rubber band and the safety pin and the matchbox. Now he had collected six things on the way to school and he was very pleased with himself. He ran into the playground feeling very cheerful.

Now you'll hardly believe it, but every single thing in Ian's pockets came in useful that day in school. It happened like this.

When Ian went into the classroom, the first person he saw was Miss Mee, watering the daffodils in their bowls. "They're getting rather tall, poor things," she said. "We'll have to tie them to a stick so they don't bend right over." She fetched a very old paintbrush that wasn't used any more.

"You can tie them with my string," said Ian.

"Just the thing," said Miss Mee, and she tied the daffodils to the stick with Ian's piece of green string.

After that Laura's skirt strap came loose. She came to show Miss Mee. "My mum'll kill me!" said Laura.

"Of course she won't!" said Miss Mee. "We'll mend it somehow." She looked round, wondering how to mend it.

"You can pin it together with my safety pin," said Ian.

"Just the thing," said Miss Mee, and she pinned Laura's skirt strap to the skirt with Ian's shiny, silver safety pin.

Not long before playtime Mary felt a bit sick. She said she felt too hot and had a headache. Miss Mee told her to sit down and rest her head on the table. "You can put my nice smooth pebble next to your head, if you like," offered Ian.

"Just the thing," said Miss Mee, and Mary thought that was a good idea too. She held the cool flat pebble next to her hot forehead. It cheered her up a lot.

During playtime Michael's tooth came out. He brought it in to show Miss Mee. She said he should take it home to put under his pillow. "I might lose it," said Michael.

"You can put it in my matchbox, if you like," said Ian.

"Just the thing," said Miss Mee, and Michael put his little white baby tooth into Ian's clean matchbox.

Afterwards they went into the playground. Miss Mee showed them how to play hopscotch on the big flagstones. "First you have to write numbers on the stones," she said. "Bother! I've not brought any chalk outside with me. Could you go inside and get me a piece, Ian?"

"You can use my bit of red brick, if you like," said Ian, showing Miss Mee his little piece of red stone.

"Just the thing," said Miss Mee and she scratched the numbers in red on the grey flagstones.

I wonder if you know what Ian had left in his pocket now?

Everyone came indoors after that. Today it was Ian's turn for painting. He loved painting and he took ages over it. When it was finished and dry, Miss Mee held it up for everyone to see, and Ian showed them the Batmobile, and Batman and Robin driving away from Catwoman. Everyone thought it was a great picture. Miss Mee rolled it up very carefully and gave it to Ian to carry home. Ian took the strong, thick rubber band out of his pocket and Miss Mee helped him to put it round his lovely picture.

"Just the thing!" said Ian and Miss Mee together, and they both laughed.

How the Whale Became

TED HUGHES

Now God had a little back-garden. In this garden he grew carrots, onions, beans and whatever else he needed for his dinner. It was a fine little garden. The plants were in neat rows, and a tidy fence kept out the animals. God was pleased with it.

One day as he was weeding the carrots he saw a strange thing between the rows. It was no more than an inch long, and it was black. It was like a black shiny bean. At one end it had a little root going into the ground.

"That's very odd," said God. "I've never seen one of these before. I wonder what it will grow into."

So he left it growing.

Next day, as he was gardening, he remembered the little shiny black thing. He went to see how it was getting on. He was surprised. During the night it had doubled its length. It was now two inches long, like a shiny black egg.

Every day God went to look at it, and every day it was bigger. Every morning, in fact, it was just twice as long as it had been the morning before.

When it was six feet long, God said: "It's getting too big. I must pull it up and cook it."

But he left it a day.

Next day it was twelve foot long and far too big to go into any of God's pans.

God stood scratching his head and looking at it. Already it had crushed most of his carrots out of sight. If it went on growing at this rate it would soon be pushing his house over.

Suddenly, as he looked at it, it opened an eye and looked at him.

God was amazed.

The eye was quite small and round. It was near the thickest end, and farthest from the root. He walked round to the other side, and there was another eye, also looking at him.

"Well!" said God. "And how do you do?"

The round eye blinked, and the smooth glossy skin under it wrinkled slightly, as if the thing was smiling. But there was no mouth, so God wasn't sure.

Next morning God rose early and went out into his garden.

Sure enough, during the night his new black plant with eyes had doubled its length again. It had pushed down part of his fence, so that its head was sticking out into the road, one eye looking up it, and one down. Its side was pressed against the kitchen wall.

God walked round to its front and looked it in the eye.

"You are too big," he said sternly. "Please stop growing before you push my house down."

To his surprise, the plant opened a mouth. A long slit of a mouth, which ran back on either side under the eyes.

"I can't," said the mouth.

God didn't know what to say. At last he said: "Well then, can you tell me what sort of a thing you are? Do you know?"

"I," said the thing, "am Whale-Wort. You have heard of Egg-Plant, and Buck-Wheat, and Dog-Daisy. Well, I am Whale-Wort."

There was nothing God could do about that.

By next morning, Whale-Wort stretched right across the road, and his side had pushed the kitchen wall into the kitchen. He was now longer and fatter than a bus.

When God saw this, he called the creatures together.

"Here's a strange thing," he said. "Look at it. What are we going to do with it?"

The creatures walked round Whale-Wort, looking at him. His skin was so shiny they could see their faces in it.

"Leave it," suggested Ostrich. "And wait till it dies down."

"But it might go on growing," said God. "Until it covers the whole earth. We shall have to live on its back. Think of that."

"I suggest," said Mouse, "that we throw it into the sea."

God thought.

"No," he said at last. "That's too severe. Let's just leave it for a few days."

After three more days, God's house was completely flat, and Whale-Wort was as long as a street.

"Now," said Mouse, "it is too late to throw it into the sea. Whale-Wort is too big to move."

But God fastened long thick ropes round him and called up all the creatures to help haul on the ends.

"Hey!" cried Whale-Wort. "Leave me alone."

"You are going into the sea," cried

Mouse. "And it serves you right. Taking up all this space."

"But I'm happy!" cried Whale-Wort again. "I'm happy just lying here. Leave me and let me sleep. I was made just to lie and sleep."

"Into the sea!" cried Mouse.

"No!" cried Whale-Wort.

"Into the sea!" cried all the creatures. And they hauled on the ropes. With a great groan, Whale-Wort's root came out of the ground. He began to thresh and twist, beating down houses and trees with his long root, as the creatures dragged him willy-nilly through the countryside.

At last they got him to the top of a high cliff. With a great shout they rolled him over the edge and into the sea.

"Help! Help!" cried Whale-Wort. "I shall drown! Please let me come back on land where I can sleep."

"Not until you're smaller!" shouted God. "Then you can come back."

"But how am I to get smaller?" wept Whale-Wort, as he rolled to and fro in the sea. "Please show me how to get smaller so that I can live on land."

God bent down from the high cliff and poked Whale-Wort on the top of his head with his finger.

"Ow!" cried Whale-Wort. "What was that for? You've made a hole. The water will come in."

"No it won't," said God. "But some of you will come out. Now just you start blowing some of yourself out through that hole."

Whale-Wort blew, and a high jet of spray shot up out of the hole that God had made.

"Now go on blowing," said God.

Whale-Wort blew and blew. Soon he was quite a bit smaller. As he shrank, his skin, that had been so tight and glossy, became covered with tiny wrinkles. At last God said to him: "When you're as small as a cucumber, just give a shout. Then you can come back into my garden. But until then, you shall stay in the sea."

And God walked away with all his creatures, leaving Whale-Wort rolling and blowing in the sea.

Soon Whale-Wort was down to the size of a bus. But blowing was hard work, and by this time he felt like a sleep. He took a deep breath and sank down to the bottom of the sea for a sleep. Above all, he loved to sleep.

When he awoke he gave a roar of dismay. While he was asleep he had grown back to the length of a street and the fatness of a ship with two funnels.

He rose to the surface as fast as he could and began to blow. Soon he was back down to the size of a lorry. But soon, too, he felt like another sleep. He took a deep breath and sank to the bottom.

When he awoke he was back to the length of a street.

This went on for years. It is still going on.

As fast as Whale-Wort shrinks with blowing, he grows with sleeping. Sometimes, when he is feeling very strong, he gets himself down to the size of a motor-car. But always, before he gets himself down to the size of a cucumber, he remembers how nice it is to sleep. When he wakes, he has grown again.

He longs to come back on land and sleep in the sun, with his root in the earth. But instead of that, he must roll and blow, out on the wild sea. And until he is allowed to come back on land, the creatures call him just Whale.

Acknowledgements

The editor and publishers gratefully acknowledge the following, for permission to reproduce copyright material in this anthology.

'The Special, Special Trainers!' by Malorie Blackman from *Betsey Biggalow is Here!* published by Piccadilly Press Ltd 1992, copyright © Malorie Blackman, 1992, reprinted by permission of Piccadilly Press Ltd; 'The Pudding Like a Night on the Sea' by Ann Cameron from *The Julian Stories* published by Victor Gollancz Ltd 1982, copyright © Ann Cameron, 1981, reprinted by permission of Victor Gollancz Ltd and Pantheon Books, a division of Random House Inc.; 'The King with Dirty Feet' by Pomme Clayton from *Time for Telling* published by Kingfisher Books 1991, copyright © Pomme Clayton, 1991, reprinted by permission of the author; 'Learning to Swim' by Stan Cullimore from *Henrietta and the Tooth Fairy* published by Piccadilly Press Ltd 1991, copyright © Stan Cullimore, 1991, reprinted by permission of Piccadilly Press Ltd; 'Hedgehogs Don't Eat Hamburgers' by Vivian French from *Hedgehogs Don't Eat Hamburgers* published in Puffin Books 1993, copyright © Vivian French, 1993, reprinted by permission of Penguin Books Ltd; 'The Sweet Porridge' by Wanda Gág from *More Tales From Grimm* published by Faber and Faber Ltd, copyright © The Estate of Wanda Gág, 1947, reprinted by permission of Faber and Faber Ltd; 'Eric's Elephant' by John Gatehouse' from *Eric's Elephant* published by Hamish Hamilton Ltd 1988, copyright © John Gatehouse, 1988, reprinted by permission of Hamish Hamilton Ltd; 'The Lonely Lion' by John Grant from *The Lonely Lion* published by Hodder and Stoughton 1992, copyright © John Grant, 1992, reprinted by permission of Hodder Headline Plc; 'How the Whale Became' by Ted Hughes from *How the Whale Became and Other Stories* published by Faber and Faber Ltd 1963, copyright © Ted Hughes, 1963, reprinted by permission of Faber and Faber Ltd; 'Ian's Useful Collection' by Margaret Joy from *Tales From Allotment Lane School* published by Faber and Faber Ltd 1983, copyright © Margaret Joy, 1983, reprinted by permission of Faber and Faber Ltd; 'The Horrendous Hullabaloo' by Margaret Mahy from *The Horrendous Hullabaloo* published by Hamish Hamilton Ltd 1992, copyright © Margaret Mahy, 1992, reprinted by permission of Vanessa Hamilton Books Ltd; 'A Surprise for Cyril!' by Shoo Rayner from *Cyril's Cat and the Big Surprise* published in Puffin Books 1993, copyright © Shoo Rayner, 1993, reprinted by permission of Penguin Books Ltd; 'New Blue Shoes' by Eve Rice from *New Blue Shoes* published by The Bodley Head 1977, copyright © Eve Rice, 1975, reprinted by permission of Atheneum Books for Young Readers, an imprint of Simon & Schuster Children's Publishing Division;

ACKNOWLEDGEMENTS

'Mashenka and the Bear' by James Riordan first published as 'Little Masha and Misha the Bear' in *Tales from Central Russia* by Kestrel Books 1976, copyright © James Riordan, 1976, reprinted by permission of the author.

Thanks to Gay Elliot for 'Billy and the Best Umbrella' by M. Joyce Davies, 'The Cock, the Mouse and the Little Red Hen' by Félicité Lefèvre and 'The Magic Scissors' by Loes Spaander – all found in her wonderful collection of early books.

Also in Young Puffin

Dick King-Smith

Be they soft and furry, sharp and prickly or smooth and scaly, all the animals in this collection are quite irresistible!

A mouse is dicing with death in the larder, while another is carried off in the jaws of a fox. Then there's a bullied brontosaurus, a wimpish woodlouse, a rebellious hedgehog and a dog with an identity crisis.

'Other writers who put words into animals' mouths are outclassed' – *The Times Educational Supplement*

Also in Young Puffin

Malorie Blackman

"OK, Terrific Twins, I have a plan."

When Maxine has a plan, you can be sure that it involves her twin brothers Antony and Edward. You can also be sure that it involves – TROUBLE!

From rescuing Syrup the cat to cooling people down at the local swimming pool, no problem is too big for Girl Wonder and the Terrific Twins. The trouble is, things never seem to go according to plan.

'. . . sparkling stories'
– *Children's Books of the Year*

Also in Young Puffin

THE LITTLE WITCH

Margaret Mahy

Some stories are true, and some aren't...

Six surprising tales about sailors and pirates, witches and witch-babies, orphans and children, and even lions and dragons!

Also in Young Puffin

Alf Prøysen

Nine delightfully funny stories about that incredible shrinking woman, Mrs Pepperpot!

How would *you* feel if you suddenly shrank to the size of a pepperpot? Well, that's exactly what happens to Mrs Pepperpot – and always at the most awkward moments. But it *does* lead her into a lot of very exciting adventures in which she meets some very unusual characters!

Also in Young Puffin

Tales of Polly and the Hungry Wolf

Catherine Storr

The wolf is no match for clever Polly!

The wolf is up to his old habit of trying to trick Polly so that he can gobble her up. He has thought of several new ways of getting her into his clutches but Polly is too clever to allow herself to be caught by a stupid wolf and she outwits him at every turn!

Also in Young Puffin

Dinner Ladies Don't Count

Bernard Ashley

Two children, two problems and trouble at school.

Jason storms around the school in a temper – and then gets the blame for something he didn't do. Linda tells a lie, just a little one – and is horrified to see how big it grows. Just as it seems that things can't possibly get worse, help comes for both of them in surprising ways.

Also in Young Puffin

Milly-Molly-Mandy Stories

Joyce Lankester Brisley

Children love to read about this enchanting little country girl!

Milly-Molly-Mandy and her friends Susan and Billy Blunt live in a little village in the heart of the English countryside. They do all the sorts of things that country children enjoy – like blackberrying, gardening and going to the village fête.

Also in Young Puffin

Poems for 7 year-olds and under

Chosen by
Helen Nicoll

Tell me, O Octopus, I begs,
Is those things arms, or is they legs?
I marvel at thee, Octopus;
If I were thou, I'd call me us.

A rich and inviting collection of verses, riddles and limericks specially chosen for children of seven years old and under.

Also in Young Puffin

Rumer Godden

"Long, long ago," said Tottie, "I knew a dolls' house. I lived in it. That was a hundred years ago."

The Plantaganets don't believe they'll ever move out of their draughty shoe-box, but then their owners are given an antique dolls' house just like the one Tottie remembers. The dolls are delighted with their new home until haughty Marchpane, a selfish china doll, moves in with them and acts as though she owns the place.

This enchanting story will thrill any child who has ever had – or dreamt of having – a dolls' house of their own.

Also in Young Puffin

NO HICKORY NO DICKORY NO DOCK

A collection of Caribbean nursery rhymes by

John Agard and Grace Nichols

Wasn't me
Wasn't me
said the little mouse
I didn't run up no clock

Well, that's what the little mouse *says*, but he's a cheeky character and always up to tricks, just like many of the other characters in this lively collection of Caribbean nursery rhymes. Join in the fun, clap your hands and chant along.

'Part chant, part song, part rhyme, the poems bowl along with a casual and easy style. This is a lovely collection for younger children'
– *Junior Education*

'No lover of poetry, whether child or adult, could fail to be entertained, enthralled, touched by these verses' – Charles Causley, *The Times Educational Supplement*

Also in Young Puffin

The Village Dinosaur

Phyllis Arkle

"What's going on?"
"Something exciting!"
"Where?"
"Down at the old quarry."

It isn't every small boy who finds a living dinosaur buried in a quarry, just as it isn't every dinosaur that discovers Roman remains and stops train smashes. Never have so many exciting and improbable things happened in one quiet village!